The HOUNDS of PENHALLOW HALL

THE MOONLIGHT STATUE

For my own William,
who helped me find Rex and the others
HW

~

STRIPES PUBLISHING
An imprint of the Little Tiger Group
1 The Coda Centre
189 Munster Road,
London SW6 6AW

A paperback original
First published in Great Britain in 2017

ISBN: 978-1-84715-660-0

Printed and bound in the UK.

2 4 6 8 10 9 7 5 3 1

The HOUNDS of PENHALLOW HALL

THE MOONLIGHT STATUE

HOLLY WEBB

Illustrated by
JASON COCKCROFT

Stripes

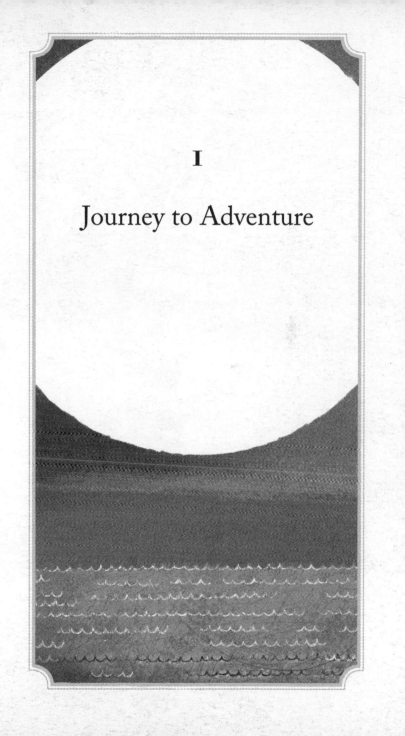

I

Journey to Adventure

Polly looked around the flat, heartbreakingly bare and empty. How could all their life have been packed up into one small van? She had loved living in London so much but now it felt as if London was forgetting them too easily. They were slipping out of the city, and no one had noticed.

It would have been different if Dad was still with them, Polly thought. She peered out of the window at her mum, who was talking to the removal man, pointing at something on her phone. Probably the map, Polly guessed.

The removal people had been a bit doubtful about how to reach Penhallow Hall. The roads all around it were tiny and twisted, Mum said, with tall hedges that leaned in, so nobody ever drove fast. It was one of the things she'd kept mentioning, when she was trying to convince Polly the move to Cornwall was a good idea. How quiet and peaceful it would be – hardly any cars, just a tractor every so often and even quite a few people riding horses.

Polly reckoned Mum was exaggerating a bit but she understood why. If they'd been living there last year, Dad would still be alive, wouldn't he? Lorries couldn't fit down those narrow little lanes, so he wouldn't have been knocked off his bike.

She shook her head briskly and the ends of her dark ponytail smacked her cheek. It made her eyes water – or that was going to be her excuse if Mum saw her, anyway.

She couldn't keep thinking about Dad. They were having a new start. From now on it would just be Polly and Mum and no one would know any different. No one would put on that fake sorry face to talk to her. No one would whisper when she walked down the corridor at school: "Did you know her dad died? He got run over on his bike."

They weren't being horrible, or they weren't *meaning* to be. But ever since January, what had happened to Dad had become the most interesting thing about Polly. The story had followed her all the way through the school year. Everyone seemed to know. School felt weird and fake, because people were so nice and careful not to upset her. Nobody was allowed to argue with her any more. Her friends seemed to be tiptoeing around her. Polly's best friend

Becca paused every time she spoke to her, as though she was checking that she wasn't going to accidentally say something awful. It made it very hard to talk about anything, let alone the important stuff. Even the teachers were being eerily kind. It seemed ridiculous to complain that everyone was too nice but that was how it felt to Polly.

Still, it was the summer holidays now. And the school down in Penhallow village went back later than London schools. She had seven whole weeks where she didn't have to explain to anyone that she only had a mum. When she started the new school, she could just say she didn't have a dad and no one would ask any questions. It would be fine. Everything was going to be fine. That was what she and Mum had been telling each other.

Polly grabbed her jacket off the windowsill and banged the door behind her without looking back.

"You didn't tell me it would be like this!" Polly gawped at the front of the house. Pale honey stone stretched on and on under the deep blue sky and what seemed like a thousand windows sparkled back at her.

"I said it was big. And I showed you pictures!"

It was true. When Mum had found out she'd got the job of House Manager, she'd shown Polly photos and brochures and even a video on Penhallow Hall's website. She'd told Polly about the building being over four hundred years old and how the Penhallows had lived there even before that. They had been one of

the richest families in Cornwall and had rooms
full of gorgeous treasures… But somehow
none of this had prepared Polly for quite how
huge and grand the house would be. They were
actually going to live here?

Well… In a very, very tiny bit of here, anyway.

"If you look sideways and behind that
chimney," Mum said, squinting at the roof,
"I think that might be your bedroom window.
Up there, look? The round one."

Polly could just about see it, tucked far away in the roof, near the top of a little turret. Somewhere deep down inside her, a spark of excitement flared. It felt strange – she had been so sad, for so long. Maybe Mum was right – they did both need something new. Polly had gone along with Mum's plan but she hadn't ever imagined it *working*. She'd been sure that the cold, dark ball of sadness in her chest was there forever. How could it not be, when Dad was gone? But somehow this ancient house was telling her, *This is going to be an adventure…*

"It's great to see you again, Anna. And really nice to meet you, Polly." Stephen handed Polly's mum a huge mug of tea and pulled out a biscuit tin. "You'll be in here a lot, I expect," he said. "Everyone meets up in the staff room when they've got a break, so there's always tea on the go, and there'll be biscuits if you look hard enough."

Polly took a custard cream, smiling. She liked Stephen – he looked scruffy in his "Penhallow Staff" fleece, with his boots caked in mud and his wild curly hair, but his bright blue eyes were friendly.

There were about twenty volunteers who ran tours round the house – part of Mum's job was to manage them all. But Stephen and Polly and her mum would be the only people

living at Penhallow all the time. Stephen
had told them how he had a cottage in the
grounds, converted from part of the stables.
As Head Gardener he had lots of people
working for him, too. But everyone went
home at six o'clock.

"Want some tea, Polly? Or squash?"
Stephen peered hopefully into a cupboard.
"Ummm, sorry... We might need to get
some in. Not sure there's been anyone
under thirty living at Penhallow for about a
hundred years!"

"Really?" Polly swung round from the
window. She couldn't stop staring. The
gardens were beautiful, lush and green in
the sunlight but, even more excitingly, she
could just catch a glimpse of the glittering sea
through the trees. "No children? Didn't the
family who lived here have any then?"

"Well, the Penhallows sold the house in the 1920s. Since then it's had quite a few owners and none of them had children. Of course it belongs to the charity now. The Penhallow

History Trust – they employ me and your mum. Perhaps you as well, when you're a bit older. There are always lots of holiday jobs, working in the café or the gift shop, that sort of thing." He grinned at her.

Polly nodded. She hadn't thought of that. It was really nice, the way Stephen seemed to see that she and her mum came as a pair. She'd been a bit worried that the other staff at the house wouldn't want her hanging about.

Stephen took a big gulp of tea. "The odd thing is, the house hasn't changed much, even though so many different people have lived here. The Penhallow family lost their son, fighting in the First World War, and they left the house. They sold most of the contents to the new owners, all the furniture and paintings and things. Since then everyone's kept it the same – because it all looks so right, I suppose. No one wanted to move things from the places they'd stood in for hundreds of years. There's even trunks and boxes of old papers and photos up in the attic still."

"It is odd that they left so much behind," Polly's mum agreed, leaning forwards eagerly. "Wonderful, though. There are some fascinating things here, it would have been heartbreaking if they'd all been taken away and sold. I can't wait to get a look at those attics. I'm sure we'll be able to find so much material up there – family photos and documents... We can set up displays! I was thinking that it would be a great way to bring the past alive for the visitors – showing how one family was caught up in world events throughout history."

Polly smiled to herself and went back to

gazing out of the window at the thin, sparkling blue line of the sea. It was nice to hear her mum sounding so enthusiastic. *We're not forgetting about you,* she promised her dad silently. *It's just … it's like the ice is melting a bit.*

"Do you like it?" Polly's mum asked. "I know it's a bit of a funny shape for a bedroom but it's because it's up in the turret."

"I don't like it, I love it," Polly told her firmly. "Look, I can see the sea from the windows on this side, and all the way down the front drive on the other. And the weird shape is fun. What's so good about a bedroom that's square?"

Her mum laughed. "I suppose so. Oh, Polly, you are all right with this move, aren't you? We're not doing the wrong thing?"

Polly whirled round and hugged her tightly.
"Of course I am. Even before I came here,
I was. And now that I've seen it – this house
is amazing, Mum. I love it that we've got our

own little flat in a turret, too – it's like a fairy-tale castle!"

"It is pretty special," her mum agreed. "There's something about it, isn't there? I know we've hardly seen any of the main rooms yet but I feel right, being here. There's a curious sort of friendliness about Penhallow, which is strange when you think how enormous it is. I feel … welcomed."

"Me, too." Polly nodded. "And it's almost ours, Mum! Did you hear what Stephen said? He has a cottage in the old stables, and it doesn't join on to the main house. It's only us that live here. After six o'clock, this is our house."

"So you fancy stretching out on the sofas in the Chinese Drawing Room?" her mum said, laughing. "Well, I'm not letting you eat your dinner off the gold plates in that huge dining room, Polly. Don't even think about it."

Polly shrugged. "I just want to explore it all, without anyone else around."

Her mum smiled. "I know what you mean," she said. "Come on – come and help me make some dinner. Let's see what our new kitchen's like to cook in. It'll be miles better than the old flat."

"That's not saying much, Mum," Polly pointed out.

"I know – the fact we'll both actually fit in it is a good start."

It was one of the nicest evenings that Polly could remember, even though she was tired from the journey and all the unpacking. She and her mum were so looking forward to exploring the house and the gardens over the summer holidays. And the beach! How could she have forgotten that? She still hadn't been down there. She sat at the little round table in the corner of the living room, resting her chin on one hand while she twirled her fork in her spaghetti.

"And there I was thinking I'd never be able to get you to go to bed tonight," her mum said, laughing. "Have you even got the energy for celebratory chocolate cake?"

"Of course I have!" said Polly but she spoiled it with a huge yawn.

"All right. But you're going to bed straight after." Mum picked up their plates and Polly watched her sleepily as she went into the kitchen and came back with a slice of delicious-looking cake.

But even though she was sleepy, she still noticed Mum glancing over at the door to the flat and to the heavy, new-looking bolt at the top of it. There was an anxious look in her eyes.

A cold chill ran down the back of Polly's neck

and the delicious sleepy feeling faded a little. Did her mum think it was going to happen here, too? Her cheeks reddening, she dug her fork into the cake quickly and tried to smile and say how delicious it was. But her voice came out flat and odd and her mum sighed.

"Sorry, Polly. I didn't mean to upset you…"

"I won't do it again," she whispered.

"It's not your fault, love. I know you don't do it on purpose. It's only because you were so upset. But in this great enormous house – I can't help worrying. If you did sleepwalk, you could end up anywhere."

"I won't sleepwalk. I promise I won't." Polly clenched her nails tightly into her palms.

"Oh, Polly," said Mum, pulling her into a hug. "I'm sure things will be better. We'll love it here at Penhallow. I know we will."

2

A Strange New Life

Polly wandered through the library, thinking over her last few days at Penhallow Hall. She ran her fingertips lightly over a shelf of leather-bound books with golden letters on their spines. Now that she'd been there for a while, she'd been introduced to most of the volunteers who ran the tours. The ladies reminded Polly of her granny Ella, always asking how she was and wasn't she cold without a cardigan on? But no one ever stopped her to ask if she was all right without her parents or if she wanted to hear the story of this suit of armour, or to tell her not to go past the barriers into the private bits of the house. It was obvious that she was different to all the children who visited Penhallow.

It sort of felt like she belonged to the house. It wasn't just the way the volunteers all smiled at her – there was something about the whole place that made her feel she was meant to be there. Polly couldn't pin it down. She spent a lot of time wandering about the rooms, trying to work out the secret. Something about the smell of the furniture polish or the flowers? But it couldn't be that. Penhallow made her feel as though she was special – that wasn't just lavender-scented polish.

Polly loved the emerald perfection of the formal gardens, too. There was a neatly mown lawn stretching out in front of the terrace, with marble steps leading down to it. Polly felt like someone out of a history book as she strolled past the two huge stone dogs guarding the steps. They were gorgeously carved, even though time had softened their edges, and Polly could see the strength of the muscles under their stone skin, as though they wanted to leap down and bound across the grass.

It wasn't only the house and gardens that were beautiful. The wild beauty of the cliffs and the rocky beach held her spellbound. But there was no one to share them with – except for her mum.

Polly frowned and then sighed. She couldn't be angry. This was Mum's big chance. An amazing job, at the very time when she needed a new start. But did Mum have to be quite so enthusiastic? She'd dived so deep into Penhallow's history that she hardly knew what year they were in, let alone what day it was. Mum had promised she'd go down to the beach with Polly soon but there was so much work for her to catch up on. Mum wouldn't let Polly swim by herself, so she still hadn't been in the water properly. All she'd been able to do was paddle.

Polly shook her head and stepped out through the little library door, the one that was hidden behind the fake books. She ducked past the volunteer explaining who all the people in the portraits were – Polly had heard the speech a few times now. They were all Penhallows, mostly from the eighteenth century, when the family had made a lot of money from mining copper. She wasn't keen to hear it all again.

She didn't have anything to do, that was the problem. There were bits of the gardens Polly hadn't explored yet but she'd had enough of gardens, even beautiful ones… She'd go and get something to read, she decided, and sit by the window in the old gallery.

She'd discovered the gallery while she was exploring the private rooms in the house a few days before. It was dusty and most of the furniture was covered in sheets but the windows looked out on to the garden – great tall windows made from hundreds of little glittering panes of glass. They had wide cushioned window seats below them, and even though the silk embroidery was threadbare and full of rips, they were deliciously comfortable.

"Look! *She's* allowed through there," someone said as Polly ducked under the red rope. "How come? I bet all the interesting stuff's back there, too."

Polly glanced back, trying not to smirk. Actually all the really nice things were in the main display rooms but she wasn't going to tell them that.

The fair-haired girl who'd
spoken was standing there with
her hands on her hips, looking
annoyed. The rest of her family,
two more fair girls who had to be
her sisters and her parents, peered
down the passageway after Polly.

"She's so lucky," sighed one of
the smaller girls.

"Couldn't we go down there?"
the littlest one begged.

Polly vanished round the corner,
grinning to herself, and raced up
the back stairs to the flat to grab
an armful of books. She eyed the
pile a little worriedly as she came
back down a few minutes later.

Mum hadn't had time to take her
into Penhallow village yet, let alone

to the nearest town, where the library was. If she raced through these, she'd be stuck with nothing to read. But at least Mum had bought biscuits – sponge fingers, Polly's favourite. Polly had four neatly lined up on the topmost book. She was set till dinner time, she reckoned.

But an hour later, she'd eaten all her sponge fingers. And she'd finished one of the books – a dog book that Mum had given her for her birthday. She'd read it before but it was her favourite – a fat book full of photographs of different breeds. It was supposed to help you find the perfect dog for you. Polly loved it but if she had a dog, she wouldn't care which breed it was. Just any dog would be amazing. It wasn't going to happen, though. They couldn't have a dog in their tiny London flat and they wouldn't be allowed to keep one here. Not in a stately home. Although that wasn't really fair, when you looked at all the dogs in the portraits.

Polly closed the book with a snap and gazed out of the window. The glass was old and thick, with a faint green tinge to it. A couple of the diamond-shaped panes had odd swirls in them, which made everything look mysterious. She pressed her cheek against the coolness of the glass, peering down at the gardens. She could see that fair-haired family, walking across the lawn and she twisted round to look at them better. The oldest girl leaped up on to the stone balustrade that ran down the edge of the terrace and turned a cartwheel along it. Polly sucked in her breath admiringly. She couldn't do cartwheels. Then

the girl jumped down and grabbed her littlest
sister in a bear hug, swinging her round and
round. Polly was sure she could hear the
little girl giggling, even from up here. All of
a sudden she ached to be down there with
them, playing silly games.

They'd stop, if she went down there, though.
That tall fair girl would probably just give her
a pitying look if she tried to join in.

"I'm like a ghost," Polly whispered to herself.
"Hardly anybody knows I'm here."

Polly knew as soon as she woke up that it had
happened again. She had that same sense of
something terribly wrong that she had felt
when she'd gone sleepwalking before. She
looked around, biting her lip. Where *was* she?
The full moon was bright but its light was

silvery and odd, and everything looked ghostly, faded to black and white by the moon-glare.

Once, back in London, she'd found herself on the pavement on the other side of the road from their block of flats in the middle of the night, with no idea how she'd got there. That was when Mum had started fussing about hiding the front door key and fitting extra bolts.

It was the same at Penhallow – Mum had made sure that the door to the flat was carefully locked each night since they'd arrived.

"She hung the key up by the door… She told me she had to in case there was a fire," Polly whispered, shivering in the cool night air. "I can't believe I got that bolt open – I must have stood on a chair."

She was standing halfway down a run of shallow steps, leading out on to a lawn, her feet bare on the cold marble. "The terrace…" Where she had seen those girls playing that afternoon.

Polly shivered again, remembering how lonely she had felt watching them laugh, and turned to look back at the house. She could see the diamond lattice of the gallery windows, glazed in silver moonlight. She should go back in – Mum might have woken up and be worrying about her – but she couldn't bring herself to move. The shining windows made the house look so different, almost unfriendly.

Polly twitched with fright and felt her nails scrape stone. She blinked, peering down at the steps. She had forgotten the dog statues, one on each side of the steps. Now she saw that she had her hand resting on the head of the huge stone hound – the right-hand dog. He had a longer nose, she noticed, smiling a little. He lay stretched out, guarding the steps with his companion on the other side.

"You're very handsome," she told him, stroking his stone head. "But enormous. I wonder what sort of dog you are. Something big – a hunting dog, perhaps?" She tried to think back to her dog book but it was hard to tell from the age-worn stone. A cloud drifted across the moon and in the dancing shadows the ruff of thick fur at the dog's neck seemed to shiver. Polly sighed. "You looked almost real then, for a moment. I wish you were. You'd come exploring with me, wouldn't you?"

She shook herself, trying to brush away the weird haunted feeling that sleepwalking left her with, and then scrambled up on to the balustrade, beside the huge stone dog. He had to be something massive, she decided, like a Great Dane, only he didn't have the right sort of face, he was too pointy. Maybe an Irish wolfhound. If he were standing, his head would come right to her shoulder. She huddled up next to him and put her arm round his great neck, pressing her cheek against the cool stone.

"You're a lot comfier than I thought you would be," she said dreamily. "You're even warm! Maybe it's just that I'm cold..."

The stone dog leaned round and nuzzled at her, blowing softly in her ear, and Polly giggled sleepily. The dog seemed to take that as encouragement. He leaned in further and licked her cheek with enthusiasm – his tongue was warm and slobbery. Polly straightened up, staring at him in shock.

Now the statue looked the same as it always had – solid and stone and very, very still. Polly shook her head and then pressed her hands against her eyes wearily. "I suppose

I fell asleep for a minute," she muttered. She gazed uncertainly at the stone dog – had she only dreamed that he'd moved? That he'd licked her? But her cheek was damp...

"Did you – did you move just then?" she said, feeling stupid. He wasn't going to answer, was he?

The great dog was still and Polly sighed. Of course she'd dreamed it. She turned away, dragging herself slowly up the steps. But as she reached the top, there was a scuffling behind her and a snort, and Polly turned round as slowly as she could.

The stone dog was standing now. He had turned round and followed her! He was peering down at Polly from the sloping balustrade, his huge feathery tail swinging from side to side and his eyes gleaming in the moonlight.

3

A Moonlight Race

Polly stood there, staring at the dog – and the dog towered over her from the top of the balustrade. Polly peered down at the place where the statue had stood – perhaps it was still there and this was another dog that just happened to be running around the gardens.

But the stone plinth was empty. On the other side of the steps, the twin dog lay gazing blankly out into the gardens, still stone.

"Do you… Do you do this often?" Polly asked. It came out in a strangled sort of whisper. "Do you come alive every night?

Doesn't anybody ever see you?" She wasn't sure if she was expecting him to answer or not. Dogs didn't talk. But then, statues didn't usually move, either.

"Not every night."

Polly gave a gasping laugh of surprise – then she pressed her hand over her mouth, frightened that the great creature would take offence and freeze to stone again in a huff.

But the dog gracefully leaped down from the balustrade and stood next to her. Now that he was standing on the ground, he came to just below her shoulder. "Only occasionally, when the moon's bright. And you spoke to me, I heard you. I couldn't resist. No one has spoken to me in a very long while. And you sounded..." He halted, shaking his scruffy, pointed ears. "You sounded as though you needed me to answer," he went on gently.

His voice was low and gruff but friendly. He sounded very much like he looked – huge and surprisingly not all that fierce.

"Yes," Polly admitted quietly, still blinking at the strangeness of a talking statue. "There isn't anyone for me to talk to here. It's just me and Mum and she's working so hard. She's almost *happy* again. I can't spoil it for her by telling her I'm lonely, not when things are working out for her at last."

"Don't you like it here? You're not happy?"
Was it Polly's imagination or did the dog
sound disappointed?

"I love it!" she said quickly. "It's the most
beautiful place I've ever seen. I love exploring
the house and the gardens. But it's not the
same, all on your own."

The dog sat down rather suddenly, his back
legs folding up like a puppet whose strings had
been cut. "No, you're right," he agreed quietly.
"It's not the same."

Polly came closer, reaching up to run her
hand over his ears. The fur there was velvet-
soft – somehow she had expected to feel dry,
hard stone. "Are you the only one that's real?"
she asked. "What about him?" She glanced
over at the other stone dog.

The huge creature nuzzled against her hand,
his head drooping. "I don't know – I don't

remember… For now I'm the only one –
perhaps for always…" He sprang up suddenly,
shaking his great head, his tail swishing from
side to side in a frenzy. He jumped on all four
paws, bouncing around like a puppy, and Polly
caught her breath in a laugh.

"Come on then!" He barked low, stretching
out his front paws. Polly would have known he
was asking her to play, even if he hadn't been
able to talk.

"Where are we going?"

"To explore! Wasn't that what you wanted?
Hurry up! Where shall we go first?"

Polly glanced back at the house, wondering
for a moment about her mum. What if Mum
woke up and found her gone? But then she
looked back at the dog, his ears quivering with
eagerness, and decided that it was worth the
risk. How could she pass up the chance to go

exploring with a stone dog? And besides, why *should* Mum wake up? She was probably fast asleep, dreaming of old documents.

The house had changed again, Polly noticed as she stared up at the windows of their flat. The otherworldly silver glare had softened to a friendly shimmer now that she had a companion – a protector.

"What's your name?" she asked. Then she bit her lip, hoping that he did have a name and that she hadn't upset him. But he turned back, gazing at her, his fat pink tongue lolling in a doggy grin.

"Rex." He cocked his head to one side, watching her. "It means king, you know." He straightened himself and gazed steadily down at her, tall and proud.

Polly nodded. It seemed right – he did look majestic. It wasn't just the size of him – his head was noble, somehow. He looked like the sort of dog who would gallop at the side of a king as he charged into battle. He looked *old*, which made his puppyish bouncing even funnier. Polly opened her mouth to ask him how old he was and then shut it again. She wasn't sure she wanted to know, not yet. It would make all this seem even more impossible. For now, she just wanted to believe.

"I'm Polly," she said, turning slowly to look around. "I don't know where we should go…" She had mostly explored the water garden so far. She loved the way the stream cascaded down over the rocks into the lake and she'd spent hours leaning over the bridge across the fishpool, watching as the huge koi carp ghosted past under her feet. But she suspected that the fish would be hard to see in the darkness. "What's your favourite place?" she asked.

The dog came to stand beside her – Polly could feel the warmth of him, pressed against her hip. "The cove. It's been so long since I felt the sand under my paws." His voice was a low growl of excitement and his tail swung against her legs. "Will you come?"

Polly swallowed. She wasn't sure about the path in the dark and her feet were bare, but she set her shoulders back and nodded. "Yes."

"Hold on to me – put your hand around my collar." There was an eagerness in Rex's voice but a note of command, too. He seemed to be quite a *bossy* sort of dog, Polly thought, blinking at the oddness of it all.

The collar was a wide band of stiff leather, studded with metal. She dug her fingers tightly underneath it, burying them thankfully in

Rex's thick, wiry coat. Some little touch of his excitement and bravery wrapped itself around her and her heart beat faster.

The great dog bounded eagerly forwards, leading her over the perfect lawn. Polly shivered, half at the eeriness of being out in the moonlit night, half with the chill of the damp grass on her bare feet. Rex paced swiftly down the flagged path to the little patch of woodland that edged the cliff. This was the wildest part of the garden – the most wild-looking, anyway. Polly had seen Stephen and the gardeners working there, trimming back the bracken from the path.

She could hear the sea now, whispering gently against the rocks of the cove. She glanced at Rex and they sped up, eager to get down to the tiny beach.

"Keep hold," he said as they came out on to

the narrow sandy path and Polly scrunched up her toes, trying to avoid the stones. The cove opened out around them as they slipped and skidded down the path, and Polly caught her breath at the glimmering silver of the water. Encircled by the rocky cliffs, the cove was sheltered from the wind. Only the tiniest waves whispered on to the shore, breaking in a mass of creamy bubbles. At the far end of the beach, a waterfall poured down a cleft in the rocks, bouncing and glittering from the top of the cliff.

Rex scuffed at the sand with his huge front paws and then turned round to look at Polly. He ducked his head a little and she stared at him, thinking that he looked almost shy. "We could run…" he suggested, flattening his ears at her hopefully.

Polly grinned. She could feel it, too – the call of that long stretch of sand, smooth and biscuity. She worked her fingers out from under his collar and pushed her toes into the sand, ready to race. She knew he'd be three times as fast as she was but she didn't care. Rex let out a wild woof and leaped away. He seemed to be halfway across the beach before Polly had even moved and she whooped, racing after him, laughing and panting and pounding over the sand.

He slowed down for her, whirling in dizzy circles after his own tail, then racing in wider circles round Polly as she ran. They ended up by the waterfall, Polly giggling and sticking her feet into the spray, and Rex bounding in and out of it, shaking water all over her.

At last they slumped down at the water line, where the sand was only slightly damp, and stared out at the sea. The moon was huge, full and round. It hung just above the water and Polly felt that if she could only stretch a little further, she could reach out and touch it, or even snatch it out of the sky to hold in her cupped hands. She leaned against Rex's shoulder, gazing dreamily at its reflection in the sea.

"We should go back," she said at last.

"Mmmm..." A soft growl.

"It's only because of my mum. I'd rather stay here with you…"

"I should probably go back, too," Rex murmured.

Polly wanted to ask if they'd do this again – if she'd see him again. But what if he said no? What if he only woke up one night a year? Or once in a lifetime? She swallowed hard – if she asked she might break the spell.

He snuffled into her ear and then whispered, "Hold on to me."

Polly wrapped her arm round his neck and buried her face in his fur. She felt the muscles in his shoulders shift as he stood, pulling her up beside him. He led her stumbling across the beach and then, at the bottom of the path, he stopped, nudging her gently. "You're worn out. Climb on my back."

"Won't I hurt you?" Polly said, swallowing

a massive yawn.

He licked her ear and panted – it made him look as though he was smiling. "No. Climb on. It'll be like old times…"

Polly was about to ask what he meant when Rex nudged her cheek with his damp nose. "Climb on," he told her firmly.

Polly gripped the thick, wiry fur at the back of his neck and wriggled gingerly up on to his back. She held on tight with her knees and gasped as Rex started to move, pacing slowly up the path. She pressed her cheek against his neck, gazing sideways at the stars scattered across the night sky like grains of sugar.

At the foot of the stone steps, Rex stopped and Polly slid slowly off his back.

"Say goodbye," he said gruffly and Polly clung round his neck even tighter.

"Goodbye."

He pulled away from her gently and leaped up on to the balustrade. Polly gasped and turned away – she couldn't bear to see him change back into a stone dog again. There was a faint scratching of paws and then a deep silence. Even the faint wind in the trees seemed to still itself and Polly raced up the steps in sudden fear.

On the top step she paused and made herself look back at him, stretched out along the stone base, his great head high. On the other side of the steps, the second stone dog stared out across the gardens in just the same pose.

Rex looked as though he'd never moved.

4

The Impossible Dream

P olly stirred and muttered to herself, pressing her face into her pillow.

"Polly love. Wake up."

She rolled over, blinking at her mum and her bedroom, confused. Her room was full of golden sunlight and she had a sense of something good, deep down inside her. Like the first day of the holidays or her birthday. She was pretty sure it wasn't her birthday, though...

"Come on, sleepyhead!" her mum laughed. "I've let you lie in but I've got to go down to the office now. You'll be all right, won't you? There's cereal and bread in the cupboard for toast. Just leave the kitchen tidy, OK? Pop in and see me later on."

Polly nodded, blinking as she woke up properly and started to remember. Rex! The beach! She buried her nose in her duvet to hide her sudden grin. Then she pulled up her feet and curled them underneath her, in case they were sticking out from the duvet. They must be filthy after the woods and the beach – she couldn't let her mum spot them. She'd worry that Polly had been sleepwalking again.

And I was, Polly realized in surprise, sitting up and smiling to herself as her mum tutted at the mess in her room and disappeared to the kitchen with the glass from the bedside table. Somehow it didn't seem to matter that she'd walked in her sleep again, not when

she'd gone out into the gardens and found...
What was Rex exactly? She'd have to ask
him... *I'll go out later – try and find a moment
when there's no one on the terrace. But I'll have
to be careful. I can't risk anyone else finding out
the secret.*

And the most likely person to notice that
something strange was going on was her
mum. If she'd got mud all over her sheets,
she'd better strip her bed and put the sheet
and duvet cover in the washing machine
downstairs.

Polly yawned and wriggled her toes, surprised
that they didn't feel sandy and grubby. Perhaps
all the sand had brushed off on the way back
up the stairs to the flat?

She yawned again and then blinked
anxiously. Had she remembered to lock and
bolt the door of the flat? If she hadn't, Mum

would know for certain that Polly had been out sleepwalking.

"Bye, Polly! See you in a bit!" The door slammed shut and Polly breathed out a long sigh of relief. She must have locked the door – although didn't remember doing it. Polly twirled a strand of hair around her fingers, thinking. She didn't actually remember coming back upstairs at all. The last picture in her mind was Rex, stony and silent once more on his plinth.

But that didn't mean her moonlight adventure hadn't happened.

Yet there was no sand anywhere – in her bed or on the floor. There was no mud on her feet and her hair felt clean – just a bit knotted like it always was in the morning. It wasn't damp, or sticky with salt from splashing in the waves. Her pyjamas didn't have any marks from the trip through the woods, either. Perhaps that was just luck – or she'd dreamed it all.

Polly swallowed, suddenly feeling sick with disappointment.

She trailed across to her window and peered down on to the gardens. She could only see Rex's grey stone muzzle – the rest of him was hidden. She couldn't really tell if anything about him had changed.

Polly sighed. It had been a dream. Of course it had. Stone beasts didn't come alive and talk.

"I suppose at least it means I didn't sleepwalk," Polly whispered to herself. But, for once, she wouldn't have minded.

Polly shifted a little, trying to ease her cramped knees. She had started out sitting on a bench just below the terrace, where she could see the two dog statues quite easily. But people kept looking at her and one lady had asked her if she was lost and needed help finding her parents. Embarrassed, Polly had mumbled something and hurried away.

So now she was perched in the yew tree, balanced in the crook between one great spreading branch and the trunk. If she peered through the dark needles, she could see Rex still stretched out on the edge of the steps. Polly didn't know what she was watching for but she couldn't drag herself away. She had been there all morning now, gazing at the statues and eyeing the visitors wandering up and down the steps. Lots of them stopped to admire the statues but no one seemed to notice anything strange about the right-hand dog. No one stroked his neck or hugged him or murmured in his ear. He looked so lonely.

Polly flinched as those two loud boys came racing up the steps again. They had been chasing each other around the gardens for ages and the oldest one had run along the balustrade beside Rex and nearly fallen off. Polly hoped he wasn't going to do it again. Although that might be a good way to wake up Rex. If he *could* wake up. She was willing to bet that he wouldn't let a child fall if he could help it. He'd grab the back of the boy's T-shirt in his teeth or something like that. Polly rolled her eyes. Now she was actually hoping that the annoying boy would fall off…

"I didn't mean it," she whispered aloud. "Oh, don't do that!"

They were climbing again, both of them this time, scrambling up on to Rex's back and pretending to ride him. *Just like I did*, Polly thought. *It still feels so real…*

The small one was kicking at Rex's sides as
if he was a stubborn pony. Polly gripped the
tree branch, digging her fingers into the bark.
*Oh, stop it! Stop it! You'll hurt him. Can't you
see you're being mean to Rex?* Even if it had all
been a dream, she still couldn't bear to watch.

She caught her breath in relief as the boys'
father strode by under the tree, waving and
calling to them to come and have their picnic.
It had to be lunchtime then. The gardens would
be quieter for a bit, as people drifted away to
fetch cool bags and rugs from their cars, or to
go to the tea room. As the boys dashed away,
Polly slid down from the tree, brushing yew
needles out of her hair, and hurried across
the grass to the steps. She reached up to Rex,
stroking the stone fur around his neck, her hand
running over the studs on his collar. She had
dreamed those, too – on the real collar they'd

been metal. "Did those boys hurt you? I wanted to tell them off." She leaned her cheek against his ears, feeling the stone scratch her skin and remembering how soft they'd been the night before. "I did think you were real." She sighed. "I so wanted you to be."

There was a faint warmth against her skin now and then the slightest of shivers ran through the stone. Polly stepped back, staring as a hint of wheaten gold rippled over the grey. It was gone almost at once but it had been there, it *had*.

"I didn't just dream you..." Polly flung her arms tightly round Rex's neck and stared into the statue's sightless eyes. "Tonight! I'll see you tonight. It'll be late. I won't be able to creep out until Mum's gone to bed. But I promise I'll come," she said under her breath.

A quiet snigger made Polly whirl round.

She stared at the statue on the other side of the steps. It had to be those boys again! Were they laughing at her?

She was so furious that they had interrupted her moment with Rex, she didn't care if she got into trouble. "Get out of here!" she yelled. "Leave us alone…"

Except there was no one there.

Polly blinked. Then she scowled and marched across the steps to peer round the other side of the dog statue. Those boys had to be hiding behind it, she'd heard them. They must have ducked down…

They couldn't have done, though.

Bushes and flowers grew right up to the steps and there was no room for even the skinniest child. The flowers stood straight and tall, the foxgloves' purple-and-white bells humming with bees.

Polly went back to stand by Rex, still frowning at the other statue. She hadn't imagined that horrible little laugh, she was sure of it. Someone had found it funny when she'd spoken to Rex. A boy, she was certain. The kind of annoying boy she knew from school, one who thought he was way cleverer than any *girl*... Polly folded her arms and glared across the steps.

And then, just for a second as the sun went behind a cloud, she saw him. A boy not much older than she was. Arms folded, like hers, and a smirk on his face. He was wearing a shirt and shorts but they were old-fashioned looking, somehow. For a start, it was an actual shirt, like school uniform, with a collar, and long sleeves rolled up. And the shorts were brown and baggy round his knees. He had battered boots on and his light brown hair was floppy and longish.

Polly caught all that in her first glimpse but what was more important was that he was most definitely laughing at her. A dog was peering over his shoulder, a great iron-grey dog, with a long muzzle like Rex. Another wolfhound. It was smirking, too, its pink tongue lolling from sharp white teeth.

"What?" Polly snapped, starting forward. "What's so funny?"

Then she swallowed, her eyes making sense of what she was seeing at last. The dog and the boy were both standing beside the opposite statue's plinth and the statue was gone.

But then the sun shone out again and there was no boy – just a statue of a dog, its stone face noble, its paws elegantly crossed. And there was no sound, except the bees buzzing in the foxgloves.

Polly was alone.

5

Footsteps

Polly lay curled up on her bed, flicking through her dog book and thinking back over the day. She was desperate to go out to the gardens again and find Rex. Rex was definitely real, even if she didn't understand exactly what he was. Something strange and magical was happening.

It was the first time she'd used that word to describe Rex, she realized. Magic. The stone dog really was magic and she was part of it. Magic was actually happening to *her*.

The thing was, if she believed in strange

stone dogs who came to life, what else might she end up believing in? Penhallow was such an old house it had to be full of stories and Polly had a feeling they didn't all end well.

She had gone back inside the house that afternoon. After she'd had that weird glimpse of the boy and the grey dog, she hadn't wanted to stay out in the gardens. She had been wandering about so deep in thought that she'd almost walked straight into Trudy, one of the volunteers, on the Grand Staircase.

Polly had apologized and Trudy had said that if Polly was at a loose end, why didn't she come and help her with the tour of the nurseries. Polly hadn't felt like smiling and chatting to visitors but she couldn't think of an excuse quickly enough.

Not many of the rooms up on the top floors were on show. One of the larger rooms had been laid out as a nursery, with the best of the toys – a huge rocking horse, a toy theatre and an amazing dolls' house full of tiny, delicate furniture. The house was made to look like Penhallow itself but only one set of rooms deep.

Trudy took out some of the less fragile pieces to show to the visitors. Polly loved the tiny beds and the fussy little dolls with their painted china faces. But at the end of the session, when they'd put all the furniture back, Trudy had stopped to answer questions. As Polly stood waiting for her in a shadowy corner of the room by the nursery door, she had been suddenly terrified.

It made her shiver even now, just thinking about it. There had been footsteps – faint, soft steps and a scratching, like claws. It was stupid to be so scared. But she hadn't been able to move, while those steps went past her...

Polly gasped, pressing a hand across her mouth as she heard footsteps again, echoing out of the darkness. And then she sighed, shaking her head. It was only Mum, crossing the passageway outside Polly's door on her way to bed. The steps paused and Polly shoved the books to one side and wriggled swiftly under her duvet, then pushed it half off again. Mum would never believe she was asleep wrapped up in a duvet on a night this warm. Polly could tell even with her eyes closed that her mum was peering round the door, eyeing her worriedly and checking that she was OK. That she was actually asleep, not about to sleepwalk across a busy road again. Although she'd have a hard time finding traffic around here.

The door shut with a faint click and Polly held her breath for a moment, waiting to hear the footsteps padding into her mum's room. How long should she leave it? Ten minutes? Fifteen? Cautiously, she wriggled her legs out from under the duvet and slid off the bed to sit on the floor. Being in bed made it all too easy to fall asleep. Even now the luminous hands on her bedside clock were blurring and fading as she stared at them...

Polly blinked and sat up, groaning. She'd slipped sideways, pillowing her head on her old toy dog. How long had she been asleep for? She peered at the clock again and sighed – it was eleven o'clock. A whole hour wasted! Still, at least that meant Mum must be asleep by now. Polly stretched her legs and eased herself up, then slipped on her plimsolls and tiptoed over to the door.

She crept down the little passage, past her mum's room and into the living room, stretching up to unhook the key. Of course, if Mum did catch her, she could pretend to be sleepwalking again. But then Mum would fuss even more about locking the doors. Polly paused, listening. All was quiet. She slipped the key into the lock, flinching at the tiny click. Mum hadn't bolted the door tonight, she must have forgotten – after all, as far as she knew, Polly hadn't been sleepwalking since they'd been at Penhallow.

Polly ran down the Grand Staircase, suddenly so excited that she forgot to be quiet. The moonlight was shining in through the tall windows over the stairs and the wooden banisters gleamed. They were made of some dark wood, worn shiny by thousands of hands. Tiny carved creatures, foxes and hounds and sharp-faced ferrets, peered out from under the banisters, lurking in between the pillars and

under the handrails. They seemed
to scurry and snap at each other in
the moonlight as Polly raced by.

She hurried past the staff room
and the offices to the little side
door. Stephen had shown her
where the spare key was kept,
attached to a magnet under one
of the pictures. Polly bit her lip –
she must have remembered that
the night before, too, when she
was asleep.

Outside in the gardens, the
moon was still almost full – just
a tiny sliver had been cut away.
The trees threw great eerie moon
shadows on the lawn and Polly
shivered. It wouldn't feel so
lonely with a dog for company.

She smiled to herself. When they'd still been living in London, she had spent ages finding out about small dogs – really tiny ones, like miniature dachshunds and teacup terriers, dogs that were so little they'd fit in a flat. She'd imagined a dog small enough to be slipped inside a rucksack and smuggled into school. And now she had a dog – or almost – and he was positively enormous. She was pretty sure that if Rex stood on his hind legs, he'd be as tall as her dad. And her dad had been six foot. Rex could have put his massive paws on her dad's shoulders. Dad would have loved it.

Polly dashed round the corner of the house to the terrace, planning to fling her arms round Rex's great neck and hug him hard. His thick fur would drive away the eeriness of the moonlit gardens. She frowned at the shadows around the steps, trying to make out the shape of the dogs, and she found herself slowing to a walk. Rex's plinth was empty. Her heart thumped – had he gone? Had something happened?

Then she squeaked as something furry nudged her elbow. "I didn't know where you were!" she gasped. "You scared me!"

"I couldn't wait any longer," Rex said happily. "I was too excited to stay still. Where shall we go tonight?"

Polly wrapped one arm round his neck, leaning against the warm, comforting bulk of him. "I've got an idea. But it isn't as exciting as the beach…" she said doubtfully.

"No matter."

"Well, could we go to the water gardens? Just to sit, maybe. I … I want to talk to you. I want to know things. I mean, are you allowed to tell me? It won't break a spell or anything?"

Rex snorted and licked her cheek. "I'll tell you

what I can, Polly. But what I know might not be all you want to hear. I haven't woken in who knows how many years, my memories are hazy."

Polly nodded eagerly, leading him down the steps and along the path around the house. The water gardens were laid out on the south side of the building, so that the Elizabethan gentleman who'd had them built could stroll around the streams and pools with his family in the warmest sunlight. Polly had read all the information boards now and heard the talks from the volunteers. She thought she could probably lead a tour of Penhallow Hall herself.

"Here," Polly suggested, leading Rex to her favourite spot on the wooden bridge. As she'd thought, they couldn't see the fish but a faint breeze stirred the night air as the cool dark water flowed beneath them, splashing over the rocks.

"What did you want to ask?" Rex leaned against Polly's shoulder. "You're very quiet."

"I don't know where to start," Polly said, sitting down and dangling her legs over the side of the bridge. "All my questions sound so stupid."

"Just ask."

"Well… What are you? I mean, how do you come alive? And when? Does there have to be moonlight?"

"I'm a dog…" Rex sounded hesitant, his deep

growl of a voice had grown thinner, almost
wobbly. Then he snorted, as though he was
laughing at himself. "I don't know what else
I am. I've been a statue for so long and nothing
else. The occasional moonlit night, when
the tide was out and the sands were calling,
then I'd wake, just for a gallop. But I always
went back to my statue before dawn." He
nudged her with his muzzle, a timid little dab
that seemed strange from such an enormous
creature. "I don't entirely remember, you see.
But I'm sure I was real once…"

Polly gasped. "Did someone turn you into
stone?" She put her hands on either side of his
head, gazing worriedly into his eyes. She had
read books where poor creatures were turned to
stone by witches or wizards or monsters, but she
hadn't ever thought of it happening in real life.

"That doesn't seem right!" Rex hung his head,

pressing it into her shoulder. "It wasn't like that. I should know…" he growled into her hair.

"I wonder how many years you've been a statue," Polly murmured. "I'm not surprised you can't think." She ran her hand down his neck, thinking of that odd glimpse of the boy and the dark-grey dog. Could Rex have seen them, too? "Does the dog on the other side of the steps ever wake up?" she asked.

"Yes." Rex pulled back, staring at her, his dark eyes catching the light. "Yes, he has in the past, I remember now. He was real once… I remember him! And the others." He stood up, pacing round her in a circle, his tail swinging heavily from side to side. Every so often he shook his ears, as though shaking away a confusing dream. "We could wake them!" he told her excitedly. "You woke me – woke me properly, I mean. Why shouldn't it work for the others?"

"Yes, but how did I wake you?" Polly knelt
up, staring at him. "I don't know how I did it.
And what do you mean, the others, anyway?
I haven't seen any more statues of dogs…
Only you two on the steps."

Rex huffed, a low, chuckling sort of sound.
He was laughing at her, Polly realized. But he
sounded so happy, she didn't mind.

"What? Why's that funny?"

"Penhallow is full of dogs, Polly. Look
around and you'll see. We're everywhere.
We always have been."

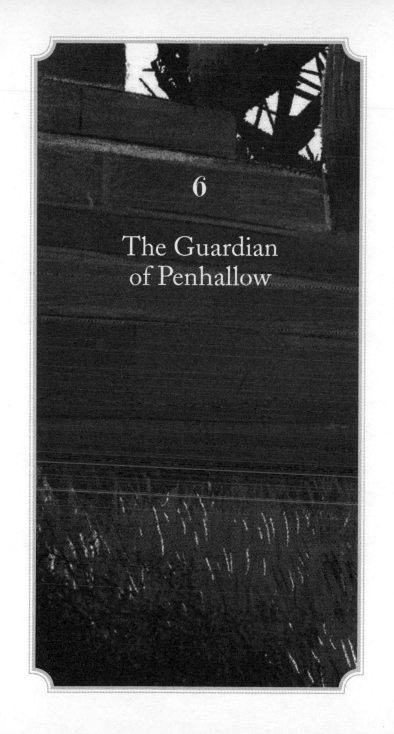

6

The Guardian
of Penhallow

Polly and Rex stood on the lawn in front of the steps, gazing up at Rex's twin statue.

"His name is Magnus." Polly felt Rex tremble as he said it. "I remember…" His eyes flickered as time and memories flooded back through him.

"Was he here when you were?" she whispered.

"No… He's not as old as I am. He lived here many hundreds of years later than I did but he played chase with me across the beach sometimes. Him and his boy." He glanced round at Polly. "I was here long before this house – and the statues – centuries before. There was a settlement here – a small knot of houses. I was just a hound then. I ran through the woods by day and at night I stretched myself out before the door of the house, guarding my family."

Polly looked at Rex's empty plinth and frowned. "I don't understand. How can the statue be you, when you lived so long before it was made?" She thought back to what she'd heard of the tours. "This house was built by Edward Penhallow in the 1600s. It's Elizabethan. But there were houses here before – there are bits left, in the grounds and down in the cellars. You're older than Penhallow Hall then?"

"Yes." He shook his ears, snorting, as though he didn't like to think about it. "Over the years the family became richer and more important. But the Penhallows still told stories about me, centuries on. That was when they gave me the name Rex."

"It wasn't your real name?"

"No one remembers my first true name. I'm the hound. They remembered me, deep down – the hound of Penhallow, their guardian. When they built this house, my family knew that I was still here. Penhallow has always had hounds. We belong here, all of us, and we stay… Here I am still. But awake now, Polly, thanks to you." Rex shook his head, his soft ears flapping. "I feel almost real again."

Polly smiled. He did seem more lively – like he had been when he'd danced across the beach. She wondered if he'd finally shaken off the stone feeling that had settled deep inside him. But she still didn't understand how he'd been stone in the first place.

"So your statue is actually a statue of you?" she asked slowly, puzzling it out. "Even though it was made ages after you … died?"

"Yes. That statue belongs to me – and it makes a good place to sleep." Rex sniffed at Magnus's paws and sighed. "Maybe too good."

Polly reached out to pet Magnus's nose. She was hoping that she'd feel the same warming of the stone and another great dog would wake up to talk to her. But Magnus stayed a statue, the rough stone chilly even in the warm night air.

"Perhaps he can't get out." Rex jumped up, putting his front paws on the base of the statue. "Magnus. Magnus, it's me! Show yourself. Come out and chase me!" He pawed at the stone, his nails scritching, but nothing happened. He dropped back down to the grass, his head drooping. "I suppose…" he murmured. "I suppose if we stay as statues for too long without waking, it may be too hard to wake again. But I'm sure I can feel him in the stone. I can smell him."

"What did Magnus look like, when he was real?" Polly asked. "Was he like you?"

"No." Rex stood a little straighter. "No, Magnus was much smaller than I am." Rex was trying not to sound disdainful but Polly could hear it in his voice. "And his coat was dark grey."

Polly nodded. She had thought Magnus was just as big as Rex but she wasn't going to say so. "But he was a wolfhound like you still?"

"Well, yes. His statue is really another statue of me but I don't need both of them, do I?" Rex pointed out, sitting down and scratching behind his ear with one huge leg. "So I let him borrow it. And of course the statues have to look like me. I am on the family crest, after all." He stopped scratching and raised one of his front paws rather dramatically.

After a moment, Polly realized that he was posing. "Oh! Yes, I've seen you. On the leaflets in the front hall. That's you?"

"Of course."

Polly nodded but she was still frowning. None of this made much sense and it didn't help that, now Rex was fully awake, he seemed to think it was all quite obvious. "I think I understand about *you* but not Magnus. Why is he still here, too?"

Rex dropped his paw and sighed. "That I don't altogether know. It's the way it is… This doesn't happen at other places?"

"Talking dogs?" Polly shook her head. "No."

"Hmmm. Well. All the dogs who've lived here – they don't leave. It's hard to explain." Rex heaved another sigh. "We belong here," he said doubtfully. "To the house and the Penhallow family – and they belong to me," he added. "Magnus and I sleep in the statues but, as I told you, there are other hounds, all over the house. Waiting to wake."

"There isn't any Penhallow family," Polly said, thinking this through. "They don't live here now. The house is open for visitors but me and Mum are the only ones who live here.

Is that why none of you wake up? Because your family's gone?"

Rex was silent for a moment, then he nodded slowly. "It must be. Before you woke me last night, it had been years. Many years, I suspect. I remember Magnus but no one after…"

He turned and sniffed at Polly, nosing at her gently, and then lifted his great front paws up on to her shoulders, so that she gasped at his weight. Then she laughed. She had never been hugged by a dog before. Rex was sniffing carefully at her hair, licking her cheeks, staring into her eyes with his own black ones.

He seemed confused. "So why did I wake for you?" Rex said. "Why did I come when you called to me? You smell right… But you say you aren't family." He dropped down again and stared at her in sudden surprise. "You're not a Penhallow?" He sniffed at her hands again.

"No. My name's Polly Morgan, not Polly Penhallow."

"Mmmf." He snorted quietly. "Who knows. You woke me. That's all that matters." He looked at her hopefully. "Would you try again with Magnus? Do what you did to me?"

Polly looked away, glad that he couldn't see her scarlet cheeks in the darkness. Mind you, he could probably smell that she was blushing – dogs could smell everything. "I'm not sure I can," she whispered. "I'll try but it won't be the same. I was so lonely. I wanted you to wake up so you'd be my friend."

Rex pressed his cold nose into the crook of her elbow and Polly jumped and then laughed.

"A child calling," Rex murmured. "A child who needed me. And living in the house, too. That would do it."

"Why a child?" Polly asked curiously and Rex gave a deep sigh.

"That was what I did. I watched the children. Protected the house, rocked the cradle, fished the little ones out of the stream when they fell in. Whatever was needed. Even when…" His voice died and Polly stared at him.

"Even when what?"

"I don't remember," Rex muttered but she was almost sure that wasn't true. There was a silence and Polly couldn't bear it.

She started to chatter, anything to break that strange, sad emptiness. "Maybe I can get Magnus to wake up, too. But I'm not lonely now, so maybe not. I can try though, can't I?"

Hurriedly she climbed up two steps and leaned against Magnus, draping her arm round his neck. "Wake up," she whispered in his ear. "Magnus, please. Rex wants to see you. So do I." She looked down at Rex. "Nothing's happening." She frowned. "Maybe he doesn't need us for company because he's already got that boy."

"What? What boy?" Rex demanded.

"I saw him today. At lunchtime. There were two little boys climbing all over your statue." She smiled as Rex growled irritably. "And when I heard laughing I thought it was one of them who'd come back. But then there was no one there – I looked. I thought maybe I'd imagined it. Then it was like the wind changed, he was just there – I saw him, a boy with a dog. A dark-grey wolfhound. It must have been Magnus."

Rex peered at her. "You saw Magnus?"

"And the boy. Could that have been his owner?"

"It can't have been." Rex leaped up to scratch at the statue again, whining pleadingly. "Magnus, listen!"

"Why not? They looked like they belonged together." Polly sniffed, remembering. "They were both smirking at me."

Rex turned back, staring at her over his shoulder. He shook his head dismissively. "No, Polly, you must have imagined it. How could you see a boy? Magnus lived here years ago – how long, I don't know, not for sure."

"I didn't imagine him…" Polly protested but even she could hear the doubt in her voice. She *had* seen the boy and the dog. But she'd seen so many impossible things in the last two days, she didn't know what to believe. "The boy had light brown hair." She frowned. "But dark eyes, dark brown. I'd forgotten that. He had these old-fashioned brown shorts on and leather boots." Polly gulped as she remembered. "Do you think he was a ghost?"

"That can't be right," Rex said.

"I know what I saw," Polly said stubbornly. "Why won't you believe me?" She folded her arms. "You're looking at me just like that boy did, as though you think I'm stupid."

"No – only mistaken." Rex jumped down. "Only the dogs remain at Penhallow, Polly. No children. I promise you."

"But if you've been asleep for years and years, perhaps it's changed," Polly argued. Why wouldn't he listen to her? "You don't know!"

"Of course I do. This is my home!"

"Well, now it's my home, too!"

Rex snorted and Polly felt her eyes fill with tears. He was right. It wasn't her house. She didn't belong at all. Not anywhere.

"I wish I'd never come here!" she cried, turning to run away up the steps.

"No! Polly, I didn't mean it. Come back!"

But she didn't listen. She raced away across the stone slabs, her plimsolls slapping, flinging herself round the corner of the house and back to the door.

"Don't you want to go out?" Polly's mum smiled down at her. "It's lovely and sunny today. You should go down to the water garden."

"It'll be full of *people*," Polly muttered,

hunching into the back of the sofa and staring down at her book.

"I suppose so." Her mum sighed. "Oh well. I came up to make a sandwich. I didn't have any breakfast, so I thought I'd have lunch early. Do you want one?"

"No. Thanks," Polly added grudgingly. It wasn't Mum's fault she was so grumpy. "I'll make one later on."

"All right. But do go down to the gardens for a bit, Polly love. You can't stay indoors all day."

Polly grunted something. She didn't want to go anywhere near the terrace and the steps.

Her mum sighed faintly and headed into the kitchen, leaving Polly feeling guilty. She couldn't be cheerful all the time, though, it just wasn't possible.

"She looks like you."

Polly sat up with a gasp and peered over

the arm of the sofa. Rex was sitting there, grinning, showing a lot of teeth and a pink tongue. He rested his nose on the sofa arm and gazed soulfully at her. "You didn't come to see me this morning."

"It's daytime! I thought you were asleep during the day. I didn't know you could be awake whenever now. And anyway, who says I wanted to see you," she added crossly. Then her eyes widened. "What about your statue? If you're up here, what happens to it?"

"Nothing. It isn't there. Because I'm here."

"That's what I mean!" Polly hissed. "People will notice!"

"Polly, did you say something?" Her mum peered round the kitchen door.

"No!" Polly shoved Rex's muzzle off the arm of the sofa and wriggled backwards, trying to hide his nose with her book.

"Oh… I was sure I heard something. Must be thinking too much about work. I've been up in the attics looking at all those boxes Stephen told us about. I found a box of the most amazing First World War letters and things yesterday, did I tell you?"

"No. I mean, yes. Good," Polly stuttered.

Mum smiled at her. "You're stuck in your book, aren't you? We're as bad as each other. Don't forget to make some lunch and *go outside!*"

She wandered past with her plate and leaned down to give Polly a kiss. Polly held her breath, hearing the faint scuffle of claws as Rex crept behind the sofa. She wasn't sure how he'd fitted round there – surely there wasn't enough room for a whole ghost hound?

As soon as her mum shut the door, Polly leaped up, leaning over the back of the sofa. A golden-brown nose flashed up and a huge tongue slathered her cheek.

"It's very dusty down here." Rex sneezed hugely and Polly giggled.

"It's a good thing you didn't do that while Mum was here, she'd never have believed it was me. And she nearly saw you!" She frowned suddenly. "Could she see you? You're not invisible?"

"I've never really thought about it…" Rex wagged his great tail. "But yes, she might have done. Your mother wasn't really paying attention, though, was she?"

Polly swallowed and shook her head. It felt like Mum never was, not recently.

"You shouldn't be up here!" she added, changing the subject. "What if someone reports your statue missing? One of the volunteers will notice, even if the visitors don't know there should be two dogs on the steps."

"I won't be gone long. I just came to tell you I was sorry." Rex hung his head, looking up at her sideways like a dog who'd stolen Sunday lunch. "I should have believed you. Perhaps there is a boy and he can help us wake Magnus? After all, what do I know? I've been asleep for years." He gave a gusty sigh. "I'll go back now – but only if you say you'll come and see me again."

"I promise. I'll come tonight." Polly flung her arms round his neck. "I'm so glad you came up here. I missed you, even if it's only been a morning."

"Me, too." Rex leaped over the back of the sofa and dabbed his nose in her ear. "Till tonight!"

7

The Boy

"What's all that, Mum?" Polly peered over her mum's shoulder at the papers spread out over the living-room table.

Her mum looked up at her, blinking. "Oh, Polly, is it dinner time? I'm really sorry, I forgot…" She ran her hand lovingly over the pile of photographs and papers on the table.

"It's six o'clock," Polly said hopefully. She had spent the afternoon in the water garden, like Mum had suggested. After Rex had come to find her, she hadn't been nearly so grumpy and she didn't even mind the hordes of people. She'd told a couple of families how to get to the beach and pointed one elderly couple in the direction of the tea room.

"Do you mind if we have pasta with sauce out of a jar?" her mum suggested. "I know it's a bit boring…"

"I *like* pasta sauce out of a jar," Polly reminded her. "You always put too many vegetables in it when you make your own." She skipped sideways to avoid being tickled and grinned at her mum. Then she stopped, looking down at the battered brown envelope that was spilling photographs over the table. "What are these?"

"They're photos of the Penhallows. You know, the people who used to own the house," her mum explained. "You can look at them if you're careful. They left so much stuff here when they sold the house, it's quite strange. I suppose it felt like ancient history. Maybe people weren't so interested in their family stories back then – or perhaps it was just a mistake that they left these bits behind." She smiled at Polly. "But I'm glad they did. It's my favourite part of my job, piecing people's lives together."

Polly brushed her hands against her shorts and carefully picked up the envelope, pulling out the handful of photos. They were brownish, all of them, and faded-looking. Polly flicked through them, trying to see what it was that fascinated her mum. The pictures didn't look that interesting to her – everyone seemed so miserable. They were all very carefully posed in groups and scowling at the camera, even the grown-ups. But several of the groups were arranged on the lawns in front of the house, she realized, smiling to herself as she saw Rex's statue gazing out at her. These were Rex's special people, she thought, looking at the faces more closely. She wondered if any of them had ever seen a huge golden dog racing across the lawns?

"Why do they all seem so cross?" she murmured, looking at one furious little girl in a frilly white dress. Actually, perhaps the girl just didn't like the dress, which made sense. It had frills everywhere a frill could possibly be stuck and the poor child had a massive bow in her hair, too.

"Well, back then cameras took so long to take a picture," her mum explained. "It wasn't a quick snap like me taking photos of you on my phone. The cameras were massive and they used these terribly expensive glass plates, one for each picture. So a photograph was a very special sort of thing and you had to sit absolutely still for … I don't know, five minutes? Or the picture would be blurred. If you went to a photographer's studio, they even had metal clamps to hold people's heads still."

"Oh…" Polly looked at the little girl again. That explained why she was so fed up, although the dress probably didn't help, either. She pushed the photos back into the envelope, and caught one small one that was about to fall off the edge of the table.

"Which is that one?" her mum asked, leaning over to look. "Oh, excellent!"

"What?" Polly looked at the photo in surprise – it was just a sepia print of a young man in a soldier's uniform, nothing very exciting.

"I've got several of him, you see." Her mum passed over another envelope. "I think I might make him the focus of one of the displays, poor boy. His name was William. That must have been taken right before he died. Yes, look. It says on the back that it's from a studio in Belgium. In 1915."

"He died? But he's really young." Polly stared at the solemn face – he was *very* young, now that she looked properly. He looked like he was a teenager. "Oh. Belgium." They'd learned a bit about the First World War at school the year before. "He was killed in the war?"

"Mmm. That's one of the reasons the Penhallows left. Remember Stephen told us on the first day? He was their only child. Perhaps they just couldn't bear the house without him… And they had no one to hand it on to, so they sold up."

Polly was looking at the other photos in the envelope. Another of William dressed as a soldier – he looked as though he was trying to grow a moustache but it wasn't going very well. A group photo of him with two other soldiers who didn't look much older than he did. *William, Bertie and Harry, 1915*, someone had written on the back in spidery handwriting. There were a couple of school photos, too – long rows of boys in striped blazers sitting bolt upright with their hands on their knees. They were lined up in front of a huge old building, covered in ivy – Polly guessed it must be a boarding school. One of them was surely William but it was hard to pick him out.

The last photo was different. Polly stood staring at it, her heart suddenly thumping so hard she felt almost sick. It was the least

posed-looking of all – it hadn't been taken in
a studio, she was sure. In fact… She turned it
over, frowning. The boy was sitting on a set
of stone steps, like the steps down from the
terrace. But it was too close up, she couldn't
see the statues to make sure. There was a
dog, though. A big, dark-furred wolfhound,
standing on the step above the boy and leaning
over his shoulder. Both of them were gazing at
the camera and grinning.

She'd seen them before. Even the rolled-up sleeves and baggy shorts were familiar. It was the boy who'd been laughing at her in the garden. He'd died... She supposed she'd known that he must have done but the photos made it seem so sad. *Why was his ghost only a boy*, Polly wondered, staring down at his grinning face. *He'd died as a soldier...*

"I've got his medals here, too." Polly's mum handed her a small leather case. "I suppose his parents were too distraught to take them... Though I can't imagine not wanting to keep everything..." Her voice quivered and Polly put an arm around her shoulders.

"I know," she said. She had a birthday card Dad had written, in a special box under her bed. A birthday card wasn't that weird but there were other things, too. She'd taken his toothpaste out of the bathroom – the pink kind that Mum didn't like. And a tiny little plastic sausage dog that he'd given her when she'd been begging for a dog of her own. She hadn't ever liked it much – she wanted a real dog, not a toy. But after he'd gone…

Polly opened the leather box and stroked the ribbons of the medals – they were beautiful, the rainbow stripes soft and faded. "He won all these?" she murmured. "Was he very brave then?"

Her mum took the box back, cradling it gently. "These three everyone got, as far as I can remember – though the Victory medal would have been sent to his parents long after he'd died." She shook her head. "But this is a special one." She pointed to a white cross, decorated with a crown and a wreath. "This is the Distinguished Service Order, I've seen it in displays at the museum. It's for gallantry in the presence of the enemy. I don't know what he did, though we might find out – I've got quite a few of his letters."

"Are you going to read them?"

"Well, yes." Polly's mum glanced up, surprised. "Of course. Letters are fantastic for finding out about family history."

"I suppose."

That boy's letters, though. Weren't they private? It seemed mean… Polly felt like she ought to go and apologize to William. If she ever saw him again. She shook her head. He'd probably just laugh at her, like last time. It felt different, though, now that she knew he was dead – and how he'd died.

Now it was clear Rex could be awake in the daytime, too, Polly decided there was no need to wait until the middle of the night to go and see him. The house and gardens closed to visitors at six, unless there was some sort of special event on, so the gardens should be almost empty. As long as they were careful, the volunteers doing the last of the tidying up weren't going to notice that she was talking to a statue.

Polly took the oat-and-raisin cookie that Mum had given her for pudding and hurried out to the terrace. It was still bathed in sunshine and the two stone dogs shone golden in the evening light. She walked down the steps almost cautiously, remembering that photo of William with Magnus. She was pretty sure that it had been taken here – perhaps on an evening just like this.

As she stood on the middle step, thinking of the smiling boy in the picture, Polly saw the faintest twitch in Rex's stone tail. She glanced round – there was no one in sight. "It's all right. You can come out."

It was the first time she had seen him change

in the daylight. The wheaten gold colour of his fur washed over the stone and his ears flickered. Then he yawned, stretching himself up on his front legs, and whisked round. His tail was swishing and his black eyes sparkled. Polly felt her mood lighten a little.

"Whatever's the matter?" Rex asked, springing down beside her. "If you were a dog, your tail would be between your legs."

"I found that boy," Polly whispered. "I know who he is – Magnus's owner."

"How?" Rex sat down, gazing at her curiously, and Polly sat beside him.

"A photograph – look, I brought it with me," she said, taking the photo out of her pocket. "I can't have it for very long, though, I have to put it back before Mum notices." Her mum had cleared everything away into a box before they'd had dinner but then she'd gone to take a long bath and Polly had slipped the photo into another envelope to bring it and show Rex.

The wolfhound peered down his long nose at the picture. "Magnus, to the life…" he muttered. "And this boy – do I remember him?"

"He died," Polly whispered. "In a war. And he was so young, look at him!"

"A child." Rex's ears drooped and his shoulders fell so that he seemed to be hunching over. "And what happened to Magnus then?"

Polly gasped. "I hadn't thought about that! Magnus must have waited for him to come home…" She turned to look at the statue on the other side of the steps. Now that she knew William's story, Magnus's long muzzle looked mournful, not grand and fierce like Rex's. "No wonder he doesn't want to wake up."

"But he has." Rex sniffed again at the statue and then nuzzled damply at Polly's ear. "I should have listened to you. You've seen them, I believe you now."

"William doesn't fit, though," Polly said thoughtfully. "It's only the dogs who stay at Penhallow, you said. Why a boy, too? And if he died in the war, why's his ghost only my age? It doesn't make sense!"

"I have no idea," Rex muttered. "It's most unusual. Quite irregular."

Polly tried so hard not to laugh at his cross, wrinkled nose that she ended up snorting out loud. "Quite irregular? You can talk! You're a ghost who's hundreds of years old and haunting a statue!"

"I don't see your point." Rex stuck his nose in the air and turned his shoulder to Polly.

"I mean, you don't exactly have a rulebook, do you?" She scooted down a step and leaned round to look him in the eye again. "Do you? I don't know, maybe there is one. *Dos and Don'ts for Ghost Dogs*. Is there?"

"No…" Rex growled, swinging his muzzle the other way so she still couldn't look at him properly. "But there are several etiquette books in the library. You could take lessons from them."

"Sorry," Polly said. She sat down on the step, carefully not looking at Rex. She hadn't meant to offend him.

"Oh, very well." He laid his nose on her shoulder. "When one has a statue and a coat of arms and a legend, one does sometimes become a little proud. Conceited, even." He scraped his claws along the stone irritably. "Why haven't I seen this boy?"

"My mother's reading his letters," Polly said. "Do you think that woke him up? Because someone was paying attention?"

Rex sighed. "I don't know for certain but I expect he has been here all along. Since he died and his parents left. I just haven't noticed. I've been neglecting my duty, I think. But now I have a child to guard again." He nuzzled her ear. "You are a very nice girl, really. I shouldn't have said that about the etiquette book."

"I don't mind." Polly closed her eyes, smiling at the faint orangey glow of sun on her eyelids and the warmth of a heavy dog's nose on her shoulder.

8

Ghost Hunting

"What are you doing out here? Are you asleep, Polly?"

Polly jumped and felt the warm bulk of Rex slip away.

"Hi…" She swallowed, trying to smile at Stephen. She didn't know where Rex had gone but he wasn't back in his statue. The stone plinth was horribly, gapingly empty. "I must have dozed off for a minute."

"Still getting used to the flat?" Stephen suggested sympathetically. "Moving's weird, isn't it? I hope you settle in soon, Polly.

It's great having you and your mum here. She's so full of ideas, it's breathing new life into the place."

Polly smiled nervously at him. She couldn't think of anything sensible to say – she was waiting for him to notice the big statue-shaped hole. She pressed her lips together hard – she was so panicked it was making her want to laugh.

"I ought to get back upstairs," she murmured. "Mum'll be wondering where I am."

"Yes, sure." Stephen was eyeing the empty plinth now. Any minute he was going to start yelling, Polly reckoned. But he didn't. He just stared at it, frowning a little. As though there was something wrong but he couldn't quite put his finger on what.

Polly wanted to scream, *Yes! I know! The statue's gone!* just to break the suspense.

But at last Stephen shook his head and smiled back. "Night then. Sleep well." And he wandered off back round the other side of the house towards the stables.

"Well, that was fortunate." Rex wriggled between the carved stone balusters, shaking lily pollen out of his shaggy eyebrows.

"You were in the flower bed? Why didn't you get back up there?" Polly hissed.

"No time. I wonder why he didn't notice that I wasn't there?"

"I thought maybe you put a spell on him! You didn't then?"

Rex snorted dismissively. "I'm not a witch, Polly, I'm a dog."

"The house did some sort of magic then," Polly said, puzzled. "He could tell something wasn't right, though. He was staring like anything. You'd better not go missing too often."

"Perhaps just occasionally," Rex agreed. "Once a day and twice on Sundays and public holidays."

"You're very silly for someone who's supposed to be a legend and a coat of arms," Polly told him, yawning.

"Can't be legendary all the time… Go home to bed." He leaped up on to the plinth. "Tomorrow you need to be wide awake. If Magnus's statue disappears again, we'll know, won't we? That they're around – then we'll go ghost hunting."

But however often they looked, the statue remained stubbornly solid and most definitely there. "Perhaps I did imagine it?" Polly said the day after, shaking her head crossly and thumping her hand on Magnus's pedestal. Then she wished she hadn't. It hurt.

But on the Sunday morning she finished breakfast and ran out on to the terrace to hug Rex. She threw her arms round his neck and then squeaked. "Rex! Wake up! Magnus is gone!"

Rex shook himself and the glorious pale gold of his fur washed over the worn stone. He leaped down from the plinth and danced around Polly, frisking and licking her like a puppy.

"Shh, shh," Polly murmured, trying to pat

him. "You can get away with being like that here, dogs are allowed in the gardens. But I think we need to go in the house – I'm sure I heard Magnus and the boy upstairs before, and dogs aren't allowed inside."

"In my own house?" Rex said, his ears flattening a little. "Oh, very well. I'll be careful. Come along then."

"It's very busy," Rex hissed, backing his way into the gap behind a huge Chinese vase. "What are all these people doing here?"

"They're looking at the house," Polly said out of the corner of her mouth, smiling sweetly at an elderly couple wandering past. "Haven't you ever noticed them before? Penhallow has been open to visitors for years and years."

Rex peered out at her, shaking his head slowly.

"No… I've hardly woken – not since the family left, I don't think. The Penhallows went away and I slept." He edged his nose around the vase again and sniffed at a man who was walking past, reading the guidebook. "Why do they come?"

"Because it's beautiful! And interesting." Polly peered up the corridor. "It's all right, you can come out now. It's a pity it's Sunday, it's the busiest day. Because lots of people aren't at work they can come on trips," she added, explaining before Rex asked. "Be quick along this bit, that's the Red Drawing Room, it's very popular. Full of Chinese carvings and things."

Rex darted a glance into the room as they scurried past, and sniffed curiously. "I remember," he murmured. "We'll go back there, Polly. I'll show you…"

But Polly wasn't listening, too busy watching out for visitors. Neither of them saw the strange blue-green porcelain dog on the mantelpiece twitch and peer after them, before settling back into stillness with a creak of china glaze.

"Didn't you see all the people yesterday? You must have come through the house to get to our flat?"

"Straight up the back stairs for most of the way," Rex said, sniffing cautiously round a corner. "Hardly saw anyone. Nothing like this! How are we going to find William and Magnus if we have to keep hiding? I can track Magnus's scent, or I *think* I can, but all these people keep getting in my way."

"This is who the house belongs to now," Polly tried to explain. "I know you think of it as still belonging to your family but it's good that everyone gets to see all the amazing things here. The visitors love your statue, you know," she added.

Rex snorted but Polly could tell that he was pleased. "I think it's safe to come out now," she said, looking both ways along the passage.

Rex was edging his way out from behind the vase when a small boy came racing round the corner. He was going so fast that he didn't see Rex – he didn't even seem to notice Polly, but then his mum came chasing after him.

Polly tried to stand in front of Rex but it was too late. He was peering curiously at the little boy, who was almost at the other end of the passage by now. Rex hadn't noticed the mum but there was no way she could miss him. Polly swallowed hard, trying to think of excuses for an enormous wolfhound…

"Sorry," the mum said as she hurried past.

"I hope he didn't bump into you?"

"Oh! No, no, he didn't." Polly shook her head, smiling with relief.

"She didn't see me?" Rex asked, wrinkling his muzzle as the lady disappeared round the corner.

"No… I think maybe you *are* invisible. After all that effort I've made trying to hide you!" Polly laughed. "Can you smell anything yet?"

"Mmmm. Up here, I think. Something's come this way." Rex padded along the small upper corridor that led to the old nurseries.

Polly quickly glanced inside the large nursery – it was full of people admiring the dolls' house and the toy theatre. "They wouldn't be in there, would they? It's too busy."

"No… But they're close." Rex sniffed the air. "Along here somewhere."

Polly shuddered. She supposed there was

no reason to be frightened – William and Magnus were only the same stuff as Rex. They were all ghosts of some kind – but the ghost of a boy, another human, seemed a lot more frightening than a dog. Rex didn't even feel like a ghost. He wasn't transparent or wispy or cold. He felt like a *real* dog. She laid her hand on his neck for comfort and he looked up at her.

"Are you afraid?"

"A little," Polly whispered. She was remembering those soft footsteps and the quiet scritch of claws. Unless there was another ghost, it made sense that William and Magnus had walked past her a few days before. But why hadn't she been able to see them? She dug her fingers deeper into Rex's fur.

"Well, don't be," Rex said. "I'm here to protect you – not that you need protecting." Then the fur along his spine rose a little and his ears tensed. "I feel them! Close by…" He stiffened into a hunting crouch and crept along the passage, leading Polly to the room at the very end. It wasn't one Polly had been in before – there was nothing on display in there.

"Open the door," Rex murmured, sniffing underneath it. The sun was shining into the room beyond, Polly could see it glowing around the door frame. *At least it's not dark*, she thought, as she wrapped her fingers round the cold porcelain door handle. Gritting her teeth, she turned the handle, pushing the door open with a grating, ominous creak.

They stood blinking in the doorway, surprised by the white light streaming through the window after the dimness of the passageway. As Polly's eyes adjusted to the light, she saw a faint movement over by the black metal fireplace. She could see motes of dust swirling in the sunlight but there was something else, too – a shimmering in the air.

"Are they there?" she whispered to Rex. His tail was beating slowly from side to side and he was staring – into the air, as far as Polly could see.

"Yes…" He moved forwards slowly, and Polly followed him, her heart thudding. As she came closer, the air seemed to settle and suddenly she saw them, as if she'd put on glasses or something had just popped into focus.

The boy was sitting cross-legged, fiddling with a clockwork train in his lap. The track was spread out in front of him, a complicated arrangement with points and some sort of turntable. The dog was slumped down beside him, half-asleep.

The boy didn't look up as Rex and Polly came further into the room. He kept his eyes on the train. Could he even see that they were there? Polly wasn't sure but she suspected that he could... That he was pretending not to see them in the hope that they would leave him alone. The way that he was fiddling with the train reminded Polly of the way she'd made drawings those last few months at school, fussing and fussing over details, long after the picture was finished. Just so that she could pretend she wasn't listening to the girls talking about her on the other side of the room.

The grey dog leaned closer to him and suddenly swiped his tongue over the boy's cheek. The boy turned away, rubbing his hand across his face to wipe away the lick and Polly realized that he was crying. Magnus had been licking at his tears.

Something shifted inside her and she was suddenly no longer afraid. She crouched down beside him. "William? What's the matter?"

He shrugged, turning away from her almost angrily, and Polly sighed. She hadn't ever wanted people to talk to her while she was miserable, so why should he?

"Sorry," she muttered. If it hadn't been for

Rex standing hopefully beside her, she would have left them alone.

"I saw you in the gardens," she said quietly. "Actually, you were rather rude, laughing at me like that. I don't know why it was so funny, me hugging Rex. You let Magnus lick your face."

The boy looked up at last. "Pretty stupid, hugging a stone dog."

"He isn't just a stone dog!"

William looked over her shoulder at Rex and shrugged. "I'd never seen him wake up. I thought it was only me and Magnus."

"You've seen me before!" Rex said indignantly. "When you were still –" he paused cautiously – "alive. I even played with you and Magnus on the beach."

"He's right," Magnus put in, barging against the boy's shoulder. "He did. I saw him."

"I might have thought I saw something.

Maybe your shadow on the sand." William peered at Rex with a frown. "But only out of the corner of my eye. I didn't think you were real."

Rex sat down, looking disgusted. "I'm beginning to think you're more special than I gave you credit for," he told Polly. "Not even family and *you* can see me."

"Who are you, anyway?" William asked her haughtily.

"I live here." Polly glared at him. "I've got just as much right to be here as you have."

William snorted and Polly rolled her eyes. She had wanted to help Rex find Magnus but the grey dog didn't seem particularly friendly and neither did his owner.

"Let's go," she said to Rex. "They don't want us. Can't we try to wake up the others instead?"

She was halfway across the room when the boy called after her. "Please don't go."

9

William's Story

"I'm sorry." William stood up, more solid now, and Polly saw his face properly for the first time – the tear-tracks in the dirt smudged across his cheeks, his reddened eyes. "I'm not used to talking to people. There hasn't been anyone, don't you see? Not in all these years. You being here – looking for me. It's made me realize how lonely I've been."

Polly nodded slowly. She wasn't sure what to say to him – how much he knew. Did he understand that he was a ghost? Did he know that he had died, and how? She wanted to know why he seemed to be a ghost her own age, when he had died as a teenager, but she wasn't sure how to ask. "I've only lived here for a few weeks..." she murmured.

"I know. I saw you come."

Polly blinked. She wasn't sure how she felt about being watched. But then it was his house, too – more than it was hers. And he had to watch hundreds of people traipsing through it every day.

"Is this your room?" she asked. "I could show you mine, if you like. I live in a flat at the top of the house. It's one of the rooms in the rightmost turret with a round window."

"I don't know if I can," he said quietly. "I stay here mostly, around the nursery. There are good memories here, you see. This is where I was happiest, before I was sent off to school. I can be in the garden, too, sometimes, when Magnus is there. But it's hard, going to other places."

Polly swallowed. She couldn't imagine mostly living in one room for a hundred years. But perhaps time didn't mean the same thing to ghosts.

Polly reached out and, almost before she knew it, she grabbed William's hand.

He gasped and tried for a second to pull away. But then he stopped and his own fingers curled around hers.

"I didn't know you could touch me," he whispered. "No one has before. No one even saw me. Only Magnus."

His hand felt cool but quite real – just like any other child. "I expect it's because of Rex," Polly suggested. "Whatever magic that makes the statues come alive works on us, too."

"It's not magic," Rex scoffed. "It's because we belong. All of us belong to the house – yes, before you tell me, Polly, I know you're not a Penhallow. I don't understand why you can see us or how you can touch William. But you have. So let's go! Adventure! Excitement! What are we waiting for? Why are we standing here talking, like little old ladies sharing a pot of tea?"

Polly bit her lip. "I only thought we could go and see my bedroom. It's not really adventurous or exciting…"

"It is for me." William grinned at her shyly. "And I'm sorry I laughed at you before. I wouldn't have if I'd known you could hear me."

Polly shrugged. "I suppose I must have looked a bit weird hugging a statue. But you'd have hugged him, if you felt like I did." She ran the fingers of her other hand through the thick, wiry fur on Rex's neck. "Do you really think that I belong here? That's why I spoke to you that first night, you know. Because I didn't feel like I belonged anywhere any more."

"You must," William put in. "I'm sure you wouldn't be able to see me and Magnus otherwise. People have come into this room lots of times over the years and never known I was here. They don't ever stay long – I suppose I make it feel strange. I've never tried actually haunting someone but they can probably tell I don't want them in here."

"So you've been here all the time and you've really never been anywhere else in the house?" Polly glanced around – the room wasn't very big.

She could walk across it in ten or twelve steps. "I thought I … I felt you, in the other nursery. Did I just imagine it?"

William shook his head. "No, you're right. There are only a few places I go – the rooms up here that I used as a child. Sometimes I'm in one, sometimes the other. Or maybe the garden. But mostly Magnus comes up here to find me. I used to sneak him up to my room – before, you know. He wasn't really allowed upstairs but my mother pretended not to notice that he slept under my bed."

Polly tugged his hand. "Just try to make yourself move. You never know." She looked round the doorway, checking for anyone else in the passage. Then she slipped out of the door and beckoned to him to follow but he stood hesitating in the doorway.

"What is it?" Polly bit her lip. Perhaps there was some sort of barrier he couldn't break. "If you can be in the gardens you must be able to get out of this room somehow."

"I know…" He put a foot out towards the door and flinched back.

"Oh, stop that nonsense." Magnus's voice was low and growly but there was something loving about it, something worried and fussy that didn't fit with his deep chest and the air of a dog about to set off on a long ramble across country.

He shook his head crossly and then jumped up, planting his front paws in the small of William's back and shoving him out into the passageway. "There," he muttered. "Could have done that years ago, if you hadn't spent all your time moping away in here."

"Why didn't you ever tell me I could leave whenever I wanted?" William stood in the passageway, staring down at his hands as though he couldn't quite believe that he was still in one piece.

Magnus loped out after him and set off along the passage. "You never tried to leave. You sat there mending that train, over and over, and I thought that's what you wanted. If we're going, we'd better go." He disappeared around the corner to the landing. "Is it up here?" they heard him call back.

"Yes!" Polly dashed after him, chasing up the stairs to the flat with Rex and William following – she could hear them, paws and boots thudding on the wooden steps, not like ghosts at all. Suddenly she found herself smiling. It was like being back home at the flat, with her and Dad deciding to take the stairs and race Mum in the lift.

She opened the door, ushering the others inside. "It's a bit small – and we haven't unpacked all the books and things yet," she said, looking around. The flat looked very bare compared to the grandly furnished rooms below. She swallowed nervously. William was used to that enormous mahogany dining table and the silver candlesticks and about six sets of knives and forks. She had been going to offer him a stale sponge finger… Although, thinking about it, ghosts probably didn't eat. "Um … I suppose it isn't anything like downstairs."

William just sniffed. "I didn't go in the formal rooms downstairs that much. So, which is your room?"

Polly smiled at him gratefully as she opened

her bedroom door. "It's here. The best bit's the round window – look. I love it."

William climbed up on to the chair Polly had set below the window, gazing out. "You can see the sea from here!"

Polly laughed. "Rex took me to the beach the first night I woke him up. I've never lived by the sea before. You're so lucky. Did you learn how to swim when you were really small?"

"Pretty young. Where did you live before you came here?"

"London." Polly shut her eyes and spoke very fast. It was still hard to say, even to a ghost. "We moved here because my dad died."

"Oh…" She could hear William shuffling his feet, as though he didn't know what to say, and her eyes snapped open. "You're a ghost! Shouldn't you be able to say something better than *Oh*? I mean, *you're* dead."

Rex snorted in shocked surprise and Polly went red. "Sorry…" William was staring at her, round-eyed. "You did know that, didn't you?" she asked panickily.

"Of course I did! I'm not stupid." He sniggered. "Just dead."

"Huh." Polly tried hard to stay indignant but she couldn't. It was actually quite funny.

"I still don't know what to say about you losing your father," William murmured. "I'd have hated it if that had happened to me."

There was a scuffling noise from the living room and then a guilty silence.

"Magnus!" William sighed as they hurried out of the bedroom. "He was probably after food. He's a dreadful thief."

"Can he still eat then?"

"No, of course not. But he likes trying. What have you done, you bad dog?" he scolded. The grey dog was looking embarrassed, standing next to a pile of papers that had clearly fallen off the table.

"There wasn't even any food up there, you awful creature." William crouched down to gather the papers and photos but he was smiling. "I can pick these things up! You don't know how strange that is." He laid the papers on the table and then Polly saw his face change. "What *is* all this?"

"My mum's research. She's putting together a new exhibition." Polly felt her throat dry up as she suddenly remembered what the papers were. Mum had got up early that morning and spread all the photographs out again. It was lucky that Polly had already slipped the one of William and Magnus back into the envelope the night before.

She darted forwards to snatch them away but it was too late. William was holding a photograph, staring at it with his mouth set into a hard line. Then he threw it down. Polly felt a tug, like a sharp gust of wind and that odd shimmer twisted in the air again.

William was gone before the photograph of him in his uniform had even landed on the floor.

The boy in the picture smiled peacefully up at Polly and she felt tears burn at the corners of her eyes.

He hardly looked any older.

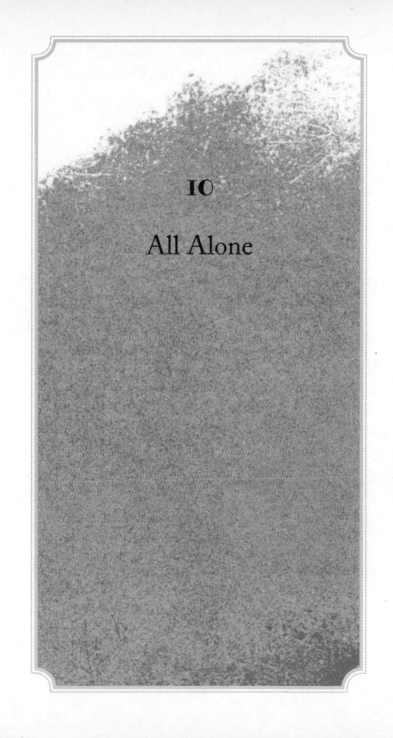

10

All Alone

Polly swung round as she heard the door handle rattle and even Rex jumped. She quickly stuffed the photographs back inside the envelope, trying to remember how all the papers had looked on the table.

As the door opened, Rex licked her hand before settling himself at her feet. Polly brushed her eyes on her sleeve. How could she have been so careless? William's story had been in the back of her mind but she had forgotten about the photographs and papers spread all over the table. Rex had been so lonely – just like her.

And now she had lost them both the chance
to make friends. She couldn't imagine that she
would ever see William again – or Magnus. It
seemed to Polly that William had chosen to
stay a child forever, safe in his happiest times,
because when he'd grown up he'd gone to war.
The photographs must have brought back the
most terrifying memories.

"Are you all right, Poll?" Her mum smiled at
her a little worriedly. "You're very red round
the eyes."

"I think I'm getting a cold," Polly muttered.
She could hardly explain that she'd driven
away one of the only friends she'd made by
reminding him exactly how he'd died.

"Oh no… Do you want to go to bed?"
Polly's mum put a hand on her forehead but
she twisted away crossly.

"No! I'll be fine, don't fuss!" The hurt

expression on her mum's face only made Polly feel worse but she couldn't stop. "I just want to be alone!"

"Polly! Sweetheart, I only want to make sure you're OK."

"You shouldn't have dragged me to the middle of nowhere then, should you? Where I don't have any friends and I'm never going to!" Even as she said it, she knew it wasn't fair – she'd hardly had any friends at home, after months of not talking to people. But why did Mum have to start fussing over her now?

It was only when she saw the golden-brown shape crawl out from beneath the table that she realized what she'd actually said. Rex seemed smaller as he crept across the room, slinking between the furniture, fading in and out of shadows so that Polly could hardly see him. He vanished round the

open door with one last
miserable glance at Polly
and she gasped, sucking
in a painful breath and
leaning over as if she'd
been hit in the stomach.

"Polly! Oh, you really
are ill!" Her mum caught
at her shoulders, trying to
look at her face.

"I'm all right! I'm going
out," Polly snapped, dimly
thinking that she had
to go after Rex. She
shouldn't have said
she had no
friends – she
hadn't even meant it. She'd
been upset, that was all.

She'd been feeling lonely for so long, they were the first words that had come out of her mouth, even though they weren't true any longer. She did have a friend. Maybe even two. Two and a half, since even though Magnus hadn't been very polite to her, he didn't seem to be nice to anyone. But now she'd driven them all away.

"You're absolutely not going out in that state," her mum said firmly. "Go and put your pyjamas on, I'll find you a hot-water bottle."

"I said I'm fine!" Polly watched with her fists clenched as her mum went into the kitchen. She obviously wasn't going to be persuaded. "Ohhhh…" Polly groaned. She couldn't stand the thought of being cooped up in the flat with Mum worrying and fussing and popping up to see her every half an hour. She darted into her bedroom, snatching up her backpack and stuffing in her swimming costume and a towel.

She'd had them ready – Mum kept promising they'd go to the beach together and swim but something always came up. Something that was more important than Polly. So she'd go by herself. She even had a book and a bar of chocolate in the backpack – she could stay out all afternoon if she wanted. Slinging the bag over her shoulder, Polly raced for the door, swinging it shut behind her with a defiant crash.

She went to the terrace first, desperate to make up with Rex – to tell him that she hadn't meant it at all. That actually, he was the best friend she'd had in ages, now that she thought about it.

His statue was back and there were visitors everywhere, admiring the flower beds, sitting on the sunny benches – there were even children climbing her yew tree. It wasn't the time for a heartfelt apology.

Polly sighed and patted Rex's nose, hoping she'd imagined that he flinched away from her. Then she set off for the wood and the path down to the beach. She'd expected it to be packed but the sun was going in – from the top of the cliff she could see fat grey clouds banking up over the sea. People were packing up their picnics and trailing back up the path as she came down.

"I don't care," Polly muttered. Right now, rain actually suited her mood. She sniffed

irritably as the first drops splashed down and headed for a small dry space under the overhang of the cliff. It would give her a little bit of shelter, anyway. She sat hunched under the rock, gazing sulkily out at the sea. When she'd looked out of her bedroom window with William, only half an hour before, it had been a glittering blue expanse – a deep, sapphire blue that sang of summer. Now it was a heaving, grey-brown mass, swelling up and then dropping down like a shaken rug.

Polly gazed at the water. She was a good swimmer. Better than Mum, actually. She'd had loads of lessons – she'd even got as far as diving, which was the top class you could do at the local pool back home …. back in London.

Suddenly she jumped up, yanking her T-shirt over her head and grabbing her swimsuit and towel out of her bag, getting ready to go in the water. She was loads better at swimming than Mum and it was stupid of her to say Polly couldn't go in. And she liked swimming in the rain. Dad always said it was the best time to swim in the sea because it made the water feel warmer. Polly had always suspected he'd just said that to cheer her up because it was raining, but still…

She raced across the beach, laughing out loud at the spatter of raindrops on her shoulders and back. She flung herself into the water –

squealing at the sudden cold but loving the silky feel as it sucked her in. She paddled out, kicking lazily, pleased to be the only one in the water. She could see for miles, it felt like. She struck out more powerfully, making for the rock just outside the bay. She'd seen people sunbathing on it before and it looked easy enough to climb up.

The cold hit her when she was about halfway. It came on gradually – she didn't realize what was happening at first. Then everything seemed to slow down. Her arms and legs were so heavy, and every stroke was an effort. Polly stopped and trod water, peering at the rock. The rain had got heavier, too. It was like looking through a grey veil. She glanced back at the shore. If she swam on to the rock, she'd have to come back again – and what had seemed a short, easy swim five minutes ago looked far more exhausting now.

She'd better turn back, she thought.

Wearily she began to swim for the beach, telling herself it would only take a minute or two. She'd go back up to the house and treat herself to hot chocolate at the tea room, the proper sort, with marshmallows and a flake. But after a few more pulls she couldn't even dream about hot chocolate – every bit of her was focused on swimming instead, dragging her aching limbs through the waves.

Then she went under. She could see it, almost as if it was happening to someone else. The dull grey water closed over her head, and she gasped and panicked and fought her way back up. But she was still so far away from the beach.

No one knew she was here, Polly realized, as she splashed and struggled to stay afloat. Even if she screamed for help, no one was coming to get her. Mum didn't know where she was.

Mum! Polly fought harder – she was beginning to see how much trouble she was in, that she might actually not be able to swim back to the shore. She couldn't do that to her mum.

Gritting her teeth, she forced her way a little further through the waves but she was so cold she could hardly feel what she was doing. Everything seemed fuzzy and dreamlike, and the sea was sucking her under again.

Then she came back up to the surface, coughing feebly. Someone was shaking her, there was yelling in her ear and teeth – *teeth* – had grabbed on to the strap of her costume.

"Stupid idiot! You shouldn't ever swim out here on your own! Don't you know about the undertow? It's really dangerous!"

Polly blinked blearily at William. He'd said he'd learned to swim, she remembered now. "Ghosts … can … swim?" she coughed out.

"Shut up and come on," he snapped back, tucking his arm under her chin. Rex had let go of her swimming costume and he and Magnus were treading water on either side of her and William. Polly wriggled trying to turn on to her front. It was horrible, stuck on her back like that, but Magnus growled in her ear and even Rex snapped, "Keep still!" So she did, staring up at the sky as William towed her back to the beach.

They'd come and got her.

"How did you even know I was here?" Polly
gabbled in between frantic teeth-chattering.
She was wrapped in her towel, and William
and the dogs were sitting facing her, all of
them glaring. They didn't seem to be nearly as
cold as she was but she supposed that was an
advantage of not being real.

"I saw you. You walked across the lawn in
front of me, didn't you? You went through
the woods to the cliff path," Rex growled. He
seemed far angrier than William and Magnus
– almost as though he couldn't look at her.
"I thought you'd come back up when it started
raining but there was no sign of you. And
then…" He slumped down, his front paws
scooting out in front of him.

"What?" Polly asked.

"It was like before," he muttered. "When you first woke me. I could feel you calling. I told you – it was my job to guard the children. Of course I heard you call."

"But I didn't." Polly shook her head. "I knew there wasn't anyone there."

"*I* was there," he said. "But you don't care about that."

"I never meant it! I just wanted to say something mean – not even to you, to Mum – because I was upset." Polly fought with the folds of damp towel, flinging them off so she could hug him. "You're the best friend I've had in ages," she whispered in his soggy ear. "Ever, I think. No, I'm sure."

Rex snorted, embarrassed, but he didn't pull
away.

"Ahhh…" William rolled his eyes and Polly
glared at him. "Hey! I saved you, too! You're
not good at being grateful, are you?"

Polly ducked her head. "Thank you. And
… I'm really sorry. About the photographs.
I forgot they'd be there. I was trying to be
friendly, showing you the flat. I didn't mean for
you to see them, I promise. I wouldn't do that."
She looked up at him anxiously, hating that he
might think she'd done it deliberately.

He shrugged and Magnus moved closer,
leaning in so that he was almost holding
William up. His dark eyes stared suspiciously
into Polly's.

"I promise I didn't," she said again, and
the grey dog rested his muzzle on the boy's
shoulder and said nothing.

"I know," William muttered. "I'd just …
forgotten. On purpose, I suppose."

Polly nodded. She didn't know what to say.
She didn't even know if he wanted to talk
about it. One day, perhaps.

They sat there in silence for a few moments,
then she whispered, "I should go. I … I have to,
I'm sorry. It's my mum. I was so angry, I shouted
at her. I can't do that, you see. She misses my
dad so much, it's not fair … me being angry."

"Not fair on you, either," William said slowly.

"No, but…" Polly shrugged. It was hard to
talk about people being gone with a ghost.

"Perhaps she needed to know what you told
her," Rex said suddenly. "I shouldn't be the only
one looking after you, should I?"

Polly clenched her nails into her palms,
suddenly feeling as though she had to defend
her mum. "It's been horrible for her," she

said. "And I don't want her looking after me too much, anyway. Just a little bit." Her voice wobbled. "Oh, I have to go!"

Polly pushed open the door of the flat, and peered round it, wondering where Mum was and how much trouble she was in. She'd only been gone a couple of hours but Mum had told her to go to bed and she'd yelled and flounced off instead. At least her hair had dried a bit – it looked like she'd just got wet in the rain. Mum wouldn't know she'd been in the sea.

"Polly!" Her mum jumped up from the living-room table. "Oh, I'm sorry! I went out looking for you, all round the gardens. I didn't know where you were."

Polly stared at her in surprise. She'd been

expecting her mum to sound cross. "I went to the beach…"

"I should have seen that you were upset about something. I haven't really been spending much time with you, have I?" Her voice sank a little as she said it and Polly dropped her bag and ran to give her a hug. "There's been so much going on – it was a chance not to think about everything, do you see? A new place…"

"It's OK, Mum,
don't worry about it. And
I'm sorry I went off like that. I'm
all right now." She let out a small sigh,
wishing she could explain what had really
been happening – about Rex and William and
Magnus, and how she felt like she had friends
for the first time in months.

The table was covered in photographs and
letters again, and Polly smiled at William and
Magnus staring up at her.

"Have you found out anything more
about him, Mum?" she asked, picking
up the photo. It had writing on
the back, she realized. *William's
eleventh birthday, 4th May,
1910.*

"I was reading
the letter his

commanding officer sent to his parents – it's so terribly sad. He died at the Battle of the Somme in July 1916 – there were thousands of men killed there on the very first day. What is it?"

Polly was staring at the date on the back of the photo. "He can't have," she murmured.

"I've got the letter – you can read it, if you're very careful."

"But look, he wasn't old enough! Not if he was eleven in 1910. He'd only have been sixteen! That can't be right, they didn't send sixteen-year-olds to fight, did they?" Polly looked at her mum, horrified.

"No… You had to be eighteen to join up and nineteen to be posted overseas. That poor boy."

Mum took the photograph, looking down at William's solemn face. "You're right! He must have pretended that he was older. A lot of boys did. They wanted to fight, you see. They were desperate to protect their country and their families."

Polly nodded. "Maybe he wanted to protect Penhallow..."

"Probably," her mum agreed, looking down at the photo of the three boys in uniform. "I wouldn't be surprised if he and Bertie and Harry were at school together and decided they'd all join up."

"Can I have a copy of this one?" Polly asked suddenly. "William and his dog?"

"I suppose so..." Her mum gave her a confused look and Polly felt she had to explain.

"He's only a little bit older than me. It's interesting – thinking about him living here.

Those are the steps down from the terrace. I've sat on those steps… I'd like to put it up on my wall." *I just wish I could have a photo of Rex, too,* Polly thought. *I suppose I could cut out the coat of arms from one of the leaflets – or I could take a picture of his statue.* But it wasn't quite the same.

"Did you meet a dog down on the beach?" her mum asked, smiling.

"What?" Polly swallowed hard, wondering how her mum knew – *what* she knew, exactly.

"You're covered in hairs! Look." Her mum reached out and took a tawny-golden hair from Polly's vest top.

"Yes." Polly smiled. "A beautiful wolfhound." She hadn't even noticed the hairs. She started to pick them off, gathering them into a little pile in her hand. She'd tease Rex when she saw him tomorrow. She'd tell him he needed grooming.

Tomorrow! Polly rested her head on her mum's shoulder. There would be so many tomorrows, with Rex and William and even Magnus. And perhaps there would be other dogs, too...

Holly Webb started out as a children's
book editor and wrote her first series
for the publisher she worked for.
She has been writing ever since, with
over one hundred books to her name.
Holly lives in Berkshire, with her
husband and three young sons. Holly's
pet cats are always nosying around
when she is trying to type on her laptop.

~

For more information
about Holly Webb visit
www.holly-webb.com